POLLEN PIE

written and illustrated by

LOUISE ARGIROFF

ATHENEUM   1988   *New York*

Atheneum, Macmillan Publishing Company, 866 Third Avenue, New York, NY 10022
Collier Macmillan Canada, Inc.

Type set by Linoprint Composition, New York City
Printed and bound by Toppan Printing Company, Japan
Typography by Mary Ahern
First Edition

10 9 8 7 6 5 4 3 2 1

Library of Congress Cataloging-in-Publication Data

Argiroff, Louise.   Pollen pie.

SUMMARY: The child of a circus family goes for a birthday dinner with her friends, a bear,
elephant, mongoose, bee, and crow, to a high-class restaurant where they proceed to drive the staff
crazy with their unusual food requests, such as beetle stew, hay soufflé, and pollen pie.
1. Circus—Fiction.   2. Restaurants, lunch rooms, etc.—Fiction.   I. Title.
PZ7.A6854Po   1988   [E]   87-3462
ISBN 0-689-31359-4

For the Stars of the
GREATEST SHOW ON EARTH—*my grandchildren,*
in order of appearance:
Shaun, Ariel and Seth Deignan;
Alexandra and Christian Argiroff;

and special friend, Valerie Jade Wydra

It was April, a very special month for Maggie.
Not only was her birthday in April, but
it was also the month that the circus
always went to the Big City.

Maggie had lived with the circus
all her life, because her parents trained
animals to do all kinds of tricks. Her father
taught lions and tigers to jump through hoops and
to balance themselves on tops of big rubber balls.
Her mother taught both little dogs and huge elephants to
dance on their hind legs and do headstands.

The circus traveled everywhere, but Maggie's favorite place
was the Big City. There were so many exciting things to do and

see there. Mostly, she loved the parade up the long avenue lined with shops and tall buildings and the crowds of people waving and cheering.

This particular April, however, Maggie was less happy than usual because the circus had arrived in the Big City the day of her birthday. That meant everyone would be so busy getting ready for the big show the next day, that there wouldn't be time for a party, nor even a birthday cake. Maggie had lots of chores to do too, and while she did them, she whistled "Happy Birthday" as loudly as she could, hoping someone would take the hint. But nobody did. They were all just too busy.

By the time Maggie finished her work, she was all whistled out and feeling quite sorry for herself. *No one cares a bit that I am ten years old today*, she thought.

Then, as though he had been reading her mind, Tovik the bear popped out from behind a pile of trunks and crates and grabbed Maggie up in a big hug. "Happy Birthday!" he growled.

Oh! Dear Tovik, I should have known you wouldn't forget!" said Maggie with a big smile.

"Neither did I," said Lobo the elephant, who had, somehow, managed to sneak up unnoticed.

"Or me either!" declared Gee-Gee the little mongoose.

"Same here!" buzzed Rosey, a honey bee who, one night, had fallen asleep on Lobo's head and, in the morning, decided to stay with the circus forever.

"Count me in, too," added Sarah the crow. "In my opinion, this is a most auspicious occasion!" Sarah loved to use big words and collected them the way some people collected stamps.

"You are positively the best friends anybody could have," said Maggie, laughing for the first time that day.

"We should have a party," said Lobo.

They all agreed.

"But where?" asked Gee-Gee. "It's like a three-ring circus around here! I was almost stepped on six times today!"

"What I need is food," said Maggie, patting her stomach.

"Me, too," grumbled Tovik. "We never eat on time when the circus is being set up!"

"Well, I have a brilliant idea," announced Sarah from her perch on Lobo's head. "Let's go to a restaurant!"

Of course!" shouted Tovik, clapping his large, furry paws together. "There must be a hundred of them in the Big City!"

"Oh, at least!" agreed Rosey. "In fact, while I was buzzing around town this morning, I saw one nearby that looked *very* high-class. A sign in the window said, THE WORLD'S FINEST CUISINE PREPARED BY ALFREDO, THE WORLD'S GREATEST CHEF.

"What is *kwee-zeen?*" asked Sarah, eager to add this grand sounding word to her collection.

"It means food," replied Lobo. Then he looked around at the circle of friends and grinned. "Well? What are we waiting for? Let's go!"

"We'll need money," Maggie said, and ran off to get her piggy bank. It was quite heavy so Lobo carried it in his trunk.

"Everyone is so busy they won't even miss us," said Gee-Gee as they trooped off.

They had walked only a few blocks when Rosey, who had flown off with Sarah, zoomed back over their heads, shouting as loud as a bee can shout, "There it is!" then buzzed off

toward a long canopy that stretched over the sidewalk like a golden roof. Along its sides, large bright-red letters spelled out THE RIK-RAC ROOM. Beneath it stood a tall man in a sparkly uniform who looked, Maggie thought, just like the leader of the circus band. He bowed slightly as they approached, then opened both doors so that Lobo could pass through with the others.

Inside the restaurant, Maggie and her friends suddenly felt very shy and stood close together near the doorway. A man in a black suit and stiff, white shirt hurried toward them rubbing his hands together nervously. His mouth looked like it was trying very hard to form a smile. "Good evening," he said. "Do you have a reservation?"

Sarah—perched on Maggie's shoulder—whispered, "Reservation?"

Whispering back, Maggie explained, "He means, did we let him know ahead of time that we wanted to eat here." She looked up at the man and shook her head. "No, Sir," she said, "but we are very hungry."

The man looked anxiously at Tovik, then said, "Wait here, please. I will have to get Mr. Polopolous, the owner of the Rik-Rac Room."

In no time at all he returned with a short, round man wearing a red flower in the lapel of his jacket. There were not more than twenty hairs on top of his pink, shiny head. "I'm sorry," he said, "but you must have a reservation."

Now, Maggie had never been one to give up easily, so she smiled her brightest smile and said, "Please, Sir, we have only just come to the Big City. We are with the circus, and today is my birthday."

Of course, everyone loves the circus, including Mr. Polopolous. His face lit up and his eyes fairly twinkled. "You know," he said, "I've always wanted to be in the circus. What a lucky girl you are. Come, follow me. We shall see what can be done."

They fell into line, with Lobo at the rear, carefully picking his way between the tables. Suddenly Mr. Polopolous stopped at a large table and snapped his fingers. Another man in a black suit and stiff, white shirt appeared. "This is Manfred," explained Mr. Polopolous. "He will take your order."

When they were seated, Manfred gave each one of them a menu. Maggie looked hers over and frowned. "Oh dear, most of the food we would like to eat is not on the menu," she said.

"Don't worry, Miss," replied Manfred. "Just tell me what you want and I'll give the order to Alfredo. He tells me, at least ten times a day, that he can cook anything."

Everyone at the table sighed with relief.

Well then," Maggie began, "we'll have a large platter of trout and a large bowl of fresh strawberries for Tovik. Sarah would like snail dumplings, beetle stew, and caterpillar cake, with raisins. Snake steak, medium rare, smothered in mushrooms for Gee-Gee. I'll have a four layer chocolate cake with ten candles on it and, lastly, a hay soufflé for Lobo. A double portion, please. His appetite is just enormous."

Sarah's word collector ears perked up. "Enormous?" she said. "What a lovely word. It must mean big."

Maggie laughed. "Yes, it means *very* big."

"Is that all, Miss?" asked Manfred.

"You forgot my pollen pie!" exclaimed Rosey from somewhere deep in the bouquet of flowers on the table.

"...And my water," added Lobo.

"Oh, yes," said Maggie quickly. "Pollen pie and a large pail of water, please, Mr. Manfred. Lobo drinks enormous amounts of water."

The waiter nodded, then hurried into the kitchen behind two large swinging doors.

Maggie and her friends settled back to inspect the surroundings. They admired the glittering crystal chandelier overhead that, Tovik said, looked like a huge birthday cake. They sniffed the mouth-watering aromas wafting through the room and enjoyed the music being played by a man strolling from table to table with a violin tucked under his chin. More than anything, they thought about the fine meal they would soon be eating. Everything seemed perfect until a high-pitched wailing sound rose up from the bouquet.

"Oh dear...oh dear...." It was Rosey, teetering on the edge of a flower petal in a cloud of pollen dust, and wringing her tiny front legs together. "We forgot to mention the nutmeg. Lots of nutmeg. Without it, pollen pie is nothing at all."

"And I would like a drizzle of honey over the strawberries," added Tovik.

Maggie stood up. "Well, I had better go into the kitchen right away and speak to the chef myself," she said, and rushed off through the swinging doors.

Moments later Manfred arrived with a pail of water for Lobo. It was very small, not at all like the huge water buckets at the circus. Lobo dipped his trunk into the pail and emptied it into his mouth with a single slurp.

In the kitchen, it wasn't hard to find Alfredo. He was the large man in a white uniform and tall white hat who was shouting, "*Snake steak?...pollen pie?* Is someone trying to make a joke on me, the Great Alfredo?"

Maggie hurried toward him saying, "Oh, no, Sir! Snake steak is Gee-Gee's favorite dish!"

Without so much as a glance at Maggie, the chef went on reading the order. His voice got louder and higher with each item. Finally, he threw up his arms and, flapping them like a giant bird, screeched, "MR. POLOPOLOUS!"

Almost immediately Mr. Polopolous appeared, smiling and rubbing his hands together as he always did when he sensed trouble. Alfredo shoved the order into his hands, demanding, "Am I supposed to cook *this*?"

Mr. Polopolous read the list carefully, then raised his head and asked, "What is the problem? Don't you know *how* to cook these things?"

Alfredo's mouth dropped open. After all, he had always claimed to be the world's greatest chef. "Of course I do. I can cook *anything*!"

"Well, then," said Mr. Polopolous sweetly, "what is the problem?"

For a moment, Alfredo was speechless. He had
never cooked snake steak or beetle stew or pollen
pie in his life, but would rather eat a farmer's
old boot than admit it. Quickly he thought of
a way to bounce the whole problem back into
Mr. Polopolous's wide lap. "It is the ingredients,
naturally," he declared smugly. "The owner of the
restaurant must supply the ingredients before the
cook can cook!"

"Hmmm...," said Mr. Polopolous,
thoughtfully stroking the twenty hairs on
top of his shiny head. "It must never be said
I have failed to do my job. Just tell me what
you need."

Alfredo snatched the order back. "To begin
with," he said, "a cup of beetles, twenty-five
caterpillars, and a snake, of course."

"Of course," agreed Mr. Polopolous pleasantly.
He went to a large sink where two men were
standing, arms up to their elbows in dishwater,
scrubbing dirty dishes. "We have a slight
problem," he said. "You both will have to go to
the park and catch a cup of beetles and twenty-
five caterpillars." Before they could say a word, he
gave each man a jar and shoved them toward the
back door, adding, "Quickly, please, and take
a lantern on your way out. It's getting dark."

Next he called to a busboy who had just come

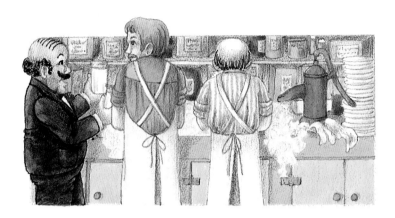

into the kitchen pushing a cartful of dirty dishes. "There's a small emergency," he explained. "We are in great need of a snake. You must go out and get one, immediately."

Where will I find a snake?" asked the bewildered busboy.

"Great gobs of goulash!! Do I have to think of everything?" sputtered Mr. Polopolous. "I don't care where you get one, just *get* one!"

"Y-Y-Yes, Sir...," stuttered the boy and rushed off.

Alfredo made a loud noise like a snorting bull and said, "It is impossible to make hay soufflé without hay. A double portion, I see."

"Better triple that," piped up Maggie. "Elephants have enormous appetites, and Lobo is very hungry."

"In that case," said the chef, "I will need two bales of hay." Then, suddenly, his eyebrows shot up. "What is *that* coming into my kitchen?" he demanded.

Maggie looked. Lobo had poked his head through the swinging doors and was sadly waggling an empty pail from the end of his trunk. "Oh, that's Lobo. He must need more water," said Maggie and rushed to get the pail.

As Lobo gave it to her he said, "I suppose they aren't used to serving elephants in the Rik-Rac Room." Then turning back into the dining room, he muttered, "I hope my hay soufflé will be bigger than the pail."

Maggie took the pail and, as she rushed off to find the waiter, almost bumped into Mr. Polopolous. He was giving instructions to the chef's helper.

"Go to the stable three blocks away, where the police keep their horses," he said. "Tell the man in charge that Mr. Polopolous needs two bales of hay. Then bring them here quickly!"

"But—" said the man.

"Tut, tut. No buts. Just bales," said Mr. Polopolous. "Two bales of hay."

The man left, grumbling loudly to himself.

Maggie found Manfred loading a tray with scrumptious looking desserts. She handed him the pail, saying, "This is so little. Do you think you could find a bigger one, please? Or maybe two this size would do. Lobo is very thirsty."

Manfred gave a tired smile and said he would see what he could do.

Meanwhile, Mr. Polopolous turned to Alfredo and said smugly, "You see? Any problem can be solved if you have brains!"

There is still the matter of the pollen pie," sniffed Alfredo. "Where is the pollen?"

"Oh, that's easiest of all!" replied Mr. Polopolous. He called to the remaining busboy and said, "Go to the flower shop across the street and tell Mr. Biddle you must have a rush order for the Rik-Rac Room."

"Roses," said Maggie quickly. "Rose pollen is Rosey's favorite."

Mr. Polopolous nodded agreeably. "Three dozen will do." He pulled a big watch out of his vest pocket, looked at it and frowned. "It's getting late," he said. "You had better hurry."

Scowling, Alfredo went to work on Tovik's order of trout and fresh strawberries. "Why can't everyone eat proper food like this?" he muttered. "Beetle stew...pollen pie...bahhh!"

"Please, Sir," said Maggie, "Tovik likes a drizzle of honey on his strawberries."

Alfredo looked down at Maggie as though he had never seen her before. "Who are you?" he demanded rather rudely, "and what are you doing in my kitchen?"

"I am Maggie," she replied, "and today is my birthday."

"MR. POLOPOLOUS!!" roared the chef. "Get this child out of here! I do not allow children in *my* kitchen!!"

Maggie had no wish to stay where she was not wanted, and was about to leave when the busboy came through the door with an armload of roses. He dropped them on one of the long tables. "I was just in time," he puffed. "Mr. Biddle was closing up for the night."

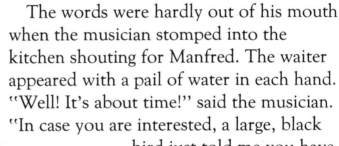

The words were hardly out of his mouth when the musician stomped into the kitchen shouting for Manfred. The waiter appeared with a pail of water in each hand. "Well! It's about time!" said the musician. "In case you are interested, a large, black bird just told me you have a customer who is fainting from thirst out there!" and he pointed a long, bony finger toward the dining room.

"Oh, dear," groaned Manfred, embarrassed, as any good waiter would be, to hear that one of his customers was unhappy.

"Hah!" snapped the musician. "It's a fine how-do-you-do when the musician has to tell the waiter where his duties lie!"

He turned to leave, but before he knew what was happening, Mr. Polopolous grabbed his arm and plopped him down on a stool in front of the pile of roses, saying, "This is an emergency. We need someone to shake the pollen out of the roses and into this bowl."

The musician turned white as a sheet and said, "But—"

"Now, now," said Mr. Polopolous, "we must all help in an emergency."

"Yes, but—," said the musician.

Mr. Polopolous insisted. He picked up a handful of roses and shook them vigorously over the bowl. "You see?" he said. "It's easy as pie. You'll be done in no time."

"I know," said the musician, "but...ah... ahhh...ahhhhhchooooo!" and to everyone's horror he sneezed, *smack!* into the bowl and the pile of roses! Pollen flew every which way! The musician opened his mouth again, "Ahhh...Ahhhhh...AHHHHHHH..." but before the sneeze exploded Mr. Polopolous grabbed a big pot and slammed it down over the poor man's head.

"...CHOOOOOOO!!" roared the musician from under the

pot. "I tried to tell you," he sniffled. "Roses always make me...ah...ahhh...ahhhhhCHOOOOOO!"

O ut! *Out* of my kitchen!!" howled the Great Alfredo. "You have ruined *everything*!"

The musician ran without even pausing to remove the pot. He went straight through the swinging doors, sneezing and knocking over a waiter and two tables on his way to the street.

T he pollen had not even settled when the dishwashers stumbled through the back door, out of breath and covered with dirt and scratches. They smacked the jars of beetles and caterpillars down on the nearest table and shouted, "WE QUIT!!"

"You *what?*" demanded Mr. Polopolous.

"WE Q-U-I-T, QUIT!!" snapped the two men.

"But—," sputtered Mr. Polopolous, "who will wash the dishes?"

"Let the beetles do them," they replied and left without so much as a backward glance.

"Boiling bilge water! This is an outrage!" roared Mr. Polopolous. His face got so puffed out and red, Maggie thought he might explode. But before he had time to, the chef pounded his fist on the countertop and bellowed, "Aughhh...wallpaper paste! This is wallpaper paste!"

Poor Alfredo! He had managed to scrape up a little pollen and mix it with flour and sugar and a pinch of this and that, but what he got, in plain words, was a very yukky tasting mess.

"Did you add the nutmeg?" asked Maggie, trying her best to be helpful. "Rosey says pollen pie is nothing without nutmeg."

"*Nutmeg!*" shouted the chef. "Whoever heard of *nutmeg* in pollen pie?"

Manfred, who had just returned to the kitchen with a trayful of dirty dishes, shrugged and said, "Whoever heard of pollen pie?"

Before the Great Alfredo could think of an answer to that, a chef's helper lurched through the door with a bale of hay balanced on his back. "Where do you want this?" he gasped.

The man staggered forward, unable to see anything but the floor under his feet.

"Come this way...this way," directed Mr. Polopolous. "No!...to the left a bit...now...straight ahead... slower...not too close to the jars...*Watch Out For The Jars!!!*"

But it was too late. Down they went with a splintering crash to the floor!

"Ohhh...great steaming stewpots!" moaned Mr. Polopolous.

"The ingredients!" shouted Alfredo in horror. "Don't let those bugs get away!"

Everyone dropped to their hands and knees except Manfred, who grabbed a broom and quickly swept the pieces of glass out of the way. The great bug chase was on!

The chef's helper's hair and shirt were bristling with bits of hay that itched terribly, but every time he stopped to scratch, Mr. Polopolous would holler, "There goes a beetle!" or "Get that caterpillar!" Finally, the man stood up and said, "This is the last straw! You catch the bugs and carry the hay! I QUIT!" and he stomped off.

"Wait!" said the busboy. "I'm leaving with you. Who can work in this crazy place?"

Unfortunately, Mr. Polopolous was so busy chasing the bugs, he didn't have time to say anything to that. After the last beetle and caterpillar in sight had been captured, he and Manfred dragged the other bale of hay inside.

Maggie decided she had better go back to her friends in the dining room. The other customers were gone by now, and even the waiters, except for Manfred, were leaving for the night. At the sight of her friends, Maggie's heart sank.

Sarah had hopped to the floor and was pecking stray crumbs out of the carpet. Gee-Gee was on a nearby table gnawing at a bone the waiters had overlooked, and Rosey had fallen asleep next to the flower bowl. There weren't any flowers in it, though. "I ate them," explained Lobo, gloomily eyeing the empty water pails beside his chair.

Maggie sighed. "Things are a bit of a mess, aren't they? But I really do think we will be dining soon. Mr. Alfredo is mixing the pollen pie and the hay has been delivered."

"I have been thinking of eating the tablecloth," growled Tovik.

There wasn't anything Maggie could say to that, so she just picked up the pails and carried them back to the kitchen for refilling.

She found Alfredo walking around the bales of hay, sizing them up. Finally he announced, "I will need at least twelve dozen eggs for the soufflé." Then he looked at Mr. Polopolous, adding, "I, myself, am too busy to get them from the storeroom."

Mr. Polopolous looked around the kitchen. Maggie and Manfred were the only other people left and Manfred was at a sink filling the pails with water. The owner of the Rik-Rac

Room threw up his hands, sputtering, "Galloping grape juice!
It seems I have to do *everything* around here!" and he stamped
off to the storeroom.

Manfred lifted the overflowing pails out of the sink and
carried them to the dining room. His shoes were so wet they
squished when he walked, and the rest of him looked frazzled
as well.

A few moments later, Mr. Polopolous came out of the
storeroom holding a huge basket filled to the brim with eggs.
Just as he was walking past the swinging doors, Manfred, on
his way back to the kitchen, gave them a push.

WHOOSH! went the doors.

CRASH! went Mr. Polopolous to the floor.

SMASH! went the twelve dozen eggs.

W hat a sight! One hundred
and forty-four eggs in slippery,
slithery gobs all over the
floor and all over
Mr. Polopolous too! He looked
like a large, raw omelette!

Manfred could hardly
believe his eyes. He stepped
forward to help Mr. Polopolous
to his feet but instead, slipped
on the eggs and went zooming
across the floor on the seat
of his pants. He came to a stop

at the feet of the busboy, who had just returned from his
search for a snake. The boy stared at him and at
Mr. Polopolous, then his forehead wrinkled into a deep scowl.

"So! A fine emergency this is!" said the boy angrily.
"While I am scouring the city for a snake, you are sitting
around taking it easy! Well, I quit!"

At the mention of a snake, Alfredo was all ears. "So?" he demanded. "Where is it?"

I couldn't find one," snapped the boy as he left, taking great care to slam the door loudly behind him.

"You are fired!" yelled Mr. Polopolous. Then he wiped his face and said he would get more eggs from the storeroom.

"Never mind!" bellowed the Great Alfredo. "I am fired! I mean, I QUIT! QUIT! QUIT!" Then he raced into the street screaming, "SNAKE STEAK! BEETLE STEW! POLLEN PIE! BAHHHHH" at the top of his voice.

"Chefs!" snorted Mr. Polopolous as he struggled to his feet. "They are all alike! Nothing but temperament! When I go to Heaven, I will have a restaurant without chefs! Do you hear? NO CHEFS!" Then he sat down on the bale of hay and burst into tears.

Manfred stood up and walked carefully through the eggs to Mr. Polopolous, sitting on the bale of hay. "What shall I tell my customers? They are still waiting for dinner."

"Tell them the Rik-Rac Room is closed!" moaned Mr. Polopolous. "Ohh...tell them I have fainted." And that's what he did.

Manfred stared at Mr. Polopolous for a long moment, then said, "I guess that is the only way to get peace and quiet in this place," and he fainted too.

The swinging doors opened and Maggie's friends stepped into the kitchen. They looked around in amazement.

"Yuk! What a mess!" growled Tovik.

"Look!" cried Lobo. "They're sleeping on my hay! The soufflé hasn't even been mixed!"

"And my snake steak!" said Gee-Gee sadly. "Not a sign of it anywhere."

"No pollen pie?" gasped Rosey.

"Nothing!" said Lobo indignantly. "There isn't even a cook!"

"This is positively preposterous!" Sarah squawked. "We should demand our money back!"

"We didn't pay them any money, and it's a good thing, too," replied Lobo, giving the piggy bank a loud shake.

Maggie sighed. "I suppose we had better go back to the circus," she said sadly.

Outside, they all climbed on Lobo's back and didn't say much on the way home. Mostly they thought about supper, hoping for leftovers at least. Maggie thought about the birthday cake she hadn't gotten.

When they arrived at the circus grounds, Tovik said, "That's funny. It's all dark. Where is everybody?"

"It couldn't be bedtime already, could it?" whispered Rosey, just in case it was.

Before Maggie could reply, she heard someone calling her name. It was her father. She slid off Lobo's back and raced toward the sound of his voice. They almost collided in front of the lion's cage. Her father scooped Maggie up into his arms.

"Thank goodness!" he said. "I've been looking all over for you."

"We're starving," Maggie said. "I hope there's something to eat."

"Well, I don't know," replied her father. "Let's go and see. Sarah, fly as fast as you can to the dining tent and tell Maggie's mother we're on our way."

They wound their way past the tents and cages and wagons to the big tent where the circus people gathered to eat. Maggie's father pulled back the flap and they stepped inside. It was very dark.

Suddenly a dozen torches burst into flame and a great chorus of voices shouted, "SURPRISE!" Then the circus band began to play and everybody sang "Happy Birthday."

Throughout the singing, Maggie was speechless. But, of course, Sarah was not. She could be heard squawking through the din. "Oh my! How absolutely, incredibly fantastic! How...how *enormous!*"

Oh, yes," agreed Maggie, grinning happily. "I knew they wouldn't forget my birthday."